Thankee
fer visitin'!

A. McWill

Ozark Night
Before Christmas

Ozark Night Before Christmas

By Amanda McWilliams

Illustrated by James Rice

PELICAN PUBLISHING COMPANY
Gretna 2004

*The word "Pelican" and the depiction of a pelican are trademarks
of Pelican Publishing Company, Inc., and are registered
in the U.S. Patent and Trademark Office.*

Library of Congress Cataloging-in-Publication Data

McWilliams, Amanda.
  Ozark night before Christmas / by Amanda McWilliams ; illustrated by James Rice.
    p. cm.
  Summary: In this version of the famous poem, Santy pays an Ozark family a
visit on Christmas Eve with his pet raccoon and gifts of musical instruments for
a fine backwoods jig.
  ISBN 1-58980-056-7 (hardcover : alk. paper)
 1. Ozark Mountains—Juvenile poetry. 2. Santa Claus—Juvenile poetry. 3.
Christmas—Juvenile poetry. 4. Children's poetry, American. [1. Ozark
Mountains—Poetry. 2. Santa Claus—Poetry. 3. Christmas—Poetry. 4. American
poetry. 5. Narrative poetry.] I. Rice, James, 1934- ill. II. Moore, Clement Clarke,
1779-1863. Night before Christmas. III. Title.

PS3613.C85O93 2004
811'.6—dc22

2003027738

Printed in Singapore
Published by Pelican Publishing Company, Inc.
1000 Burmaster Street, Gretna, Louisiana 70053

OZARK NIGHT BEFORE CHRISTMAS

'Twere Christmas Eve, an' mist a-crept off the crick.
An' the col' winner drizzly was a-comin' down thick.

Crick—Creek.

Snores o' thunder rattl't from Paw an' Maw,
But I lay wake t' ketch Santy, with m' dawg Arkansaw.
We-uns kep' up all evenin', past midnight I reckin,
When that coonhound jump't up, a-sniffin' out sumpthin'.

I foller't 'im down the holler, whar a-paddlin' the crick,
Well bedog m' cats, iffen it wharn't ol' Saint Nick!

*Holler—Hollow, the low dip between mountains, generally
cut by a creek that runs through it.*

He was a-sportin' overhalls an' a tatter't felt hat.
Outer his wild white beard peep't a little black bat.
A-top Santy's shoulder, like he was a-tree't,
Was the whoppery-ist raccoon what I ever see't.

Santy spy't us an' said, "By sassafrack!
Don't jest stand thar a-gapin'. Come he'p pack a sack!"

Back at the cabin, Maw an' Paw were a-skiddle,
A-hoppin' 'round the perch lak spiders 'top a griddle.
Paw had him his shotgun an' was a-wavin' hit 'roun'.
I holler't, "Tarnation, put that devil't thang down!
We ain't no Bald Knobbers comin' t' do you unpleasint!
Cain't you see hit's Santy a-comin' with presints?"

*Bald Knobbers—Gangs of bandits who routinely robbed
their neighbors during and after the Civil War.*

Maw said, "Well howdy! Come an' rest by the fahr.
Bring yer varmints in too. You-uns mus' be bone tarr."
"Now jest whoa thar, Santy," Paw said with a grin.
"Hain't thar a spee-cific way you-uns s'pose t' git in?"
"By hick'ry, yer roof's high as cats' backs, mebbe more.
An' yer chimbley's might narr' . . . I'm all fer yer door!"

Santy troop't right in 'er cabin, the coon a-flittin' 'is tail,
'Til Arkansaw tuck after 'im with a hot-blooded wail.

Them jokey-fied rascals lak chain lightnin' a-race't,
Tore up Maw's cook room, done busted the place!

Cook room—Kitchen.
Jokey-fied—Not right in the head.

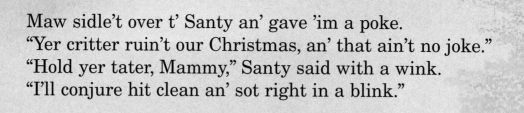

Maw sidle't over t' Santy an' gave 'im a poke.
"Yer critter ruin't our Christmas, an' that ain't no joke."
"Hold yer tater, Mammy," Santy said with a wink.
"I'll conjure hit clean an' sot right in a blink."

Conjure—To use magic.

He whistle't a note, made it tidy as a
    preacher's livin'.
An' a fine ham-biscuit feast were lai't
    out in 'er kitchen.
Right up we-uns et it, lef' nar' a
    crumb,
Then retire't to the fahrboard, whar 'er
    stockins was hung.

*Fahrboard—Fireboard, a fireplace's
mantle.*

Maw reach't in a hand. She was plumb thunderstruck,
'Cause a bran' new g'itar in 'er sock was tuck't!

Fer me t'were a dulcymore, with
  sich a soft sound
Hit whar soundin' lak raindrops
  a-tricklin' down.

*Dulcymore—Dulcimer; traditional string instrument
with strings stretched over a sounding board, played
by striking with small "hammers."*

Fer Paw t'was a fiddle to tuck under his chin.
He pick't up the bow an' the music begin.

Santy kick't up his heels in a fine backwoods jig.
I 'low hit whar a scene would make ary heart big.

Jig—Traditional dance, Scots-Irish origin.

Soon Paw said, "I's a-frolicated all one man can."
He sot down his fiddle an' plopp't on the didvan.
Santy said, "Hit's been a hoot, but folkses, I got t' git.
Thar's a heap more cabins what I got t' hit."

Didvan—Divan, sofa.
Frolicate—To make merry, dance, party.

Paw said, "Thankee, Santy, fer a-callin' up on 'er knob."
Santy said, "Shucks, folks, jest a-doin' m' job."
He hike't up his galluses, pick't up his sack,
Whistle't up his critter, an' headed down the track.

Galluses—Straps for keeping one's pants up, suspenders or
  the straps on overalls, often attached with a bent nail.
Knob—The slope and/or peak of a mountain.

And I heer't him a-call, as he floated through the night,
"Happy Christmas to all, ev'ry maw, paw, 'n tyke!"